Diane Goode's CHRISTMAS MAGIC

POEMS AND CAROLS

A Random House PICTUREBACK®

With special thanks to Bobbi Katz

ACKNOWLEDGMENTS

Grateful acknowledgment is made to the following for permission to reprint the copyrighted material listed below:

Bookstop Literary Agency for "Gingerbread House" and "The Christmas Stocking" by Dee Lillegard. Copyright © 1992 by Dee Lillegard.

Checkerboard Press, Inc., for "Duckle, Duckle, Daisy," from *The Peter Patter Book of Nursery Rhymes* by Leroy F. Jackson. Copyright 1918, 1946 by Checkerboard Press, Inc.

Aileen Fisher for "Now December's Here" and "Suddenly." Reprinted by permission of the author, who controls all rights.

GRM Associates, Inc., for "Under the Mistletoe," from the book *Copper Sun* by Countee Cullen. Copyright 1927 by Harper & Brothers; copyright renewed 1955 by Ida M. Cullen. Reprinted by permission of GRM Associates, Inc., Agents for the Estate of Ida M. Cullen.

HarperCollins Publishers for "In the Week When Christmas Comes," from *Eleanor Farjeon's Poems for Children* by Eleanor Farjeon. Copyright 1927, renewed 1955 by Eleanor Farjeon. Reprinted by permission of HarperCollins Publishers. British rights exclusive of Canada administered by Harold Ober Associates, Inc.

Bobbi Katz for "Christmas Present." Copyright © 1992 by Bobbi Katz, who controls all rights.

Alfred A. Knopf, Inc., for "December," by John Updike, from *A Child's Calendar* by John Updike and Nancy Burkert. Copyright © 1965 by John Updike and Nancy Burkert. Reprinted by permission of Alfred A. Knopf, Inc.

Constance Levy for "Two Trees." Copyright © 1992 by Constance Levy.

Harold Ober Associates, Inc., for "Shepherd's Song at Christmas" by Langston Hughes. Copyright © 1958 by Langston Hughes. Copyright renewed 1986 by George Houston Bass. Reprinted by permission of Harold Ober Associates, Inc.

Library of Congress Cataloging-in-Publication Data

Diane Goode's Christmas magic : poems and carols / illustrated by Diane Goode.
    p.   cm. — (Random House pictureback)
  Summary: A collection of traditional and modern Christmas poems and carols.
  ISBN 0-679-82427-8 (pbk.) — ISBN 0-679-92427-2 (lib. bdg.)
  1. Christmas—Juvenile poetry. 2. Carols—Texts—Juvenile literature. 3. Christmas music. [1. Christmas—Poetry. 2. Poetry—Collections. 3. Carols.] I. Goode, Diane, ill.
PN6110.C5D48 1992
808.81'933—dc20   92-6366

Manufactured in the United States of America

10 9 8 7 6 5 4 3 2 1

Diane Goode's CHRISTMAS MAGIC

POEMS AND CAROLS

RANDOM HOUSE 🏠 NEW YORK

December

First snow! The flakes,
    So few, so light,
Remake the world
    In solid white.

All bundled up,
    We feel as if
We were fat penguins,
    Warm and stiff.

Downtown, the stores
    Half split their sides,
And Mother brings home
    Things she hides.

Old carols peal.
      The dusk is dense.
There is a mood
      Of sweet suspense.

The shepherds wait,
      The kings, the tree—
All wait for something
      Yet to be,

Some miracle.
      And then it's here,
Wrapped up in hope—
      Another year!

John Updike

Suddenly

Suddenly the shops are bright,
changed by magic overnight —
red and green against the white.

Suddenly the streets are gay
as the carols begin to play
up and down, across the way.

And the children, young and old,
ruddy with December cold,
suddenly are good as gold.

Aileen Fisher

Before Christmas

Young trees of the forest,
By scores and by dozens,
Have come to the city
Like small country cousins.

On squares and on corners
They lend to each street
A strange kind of fragrance
That's spicy and sweet.

So give them a welcome,
Be glad we are blessed
For even a season
With such sturdy guests.

Anne Blackwell Payne

Two Trees

They are dressing the tallest tree
in the city square
to light tonight.
A silver star shines
on its tip.
Now they are draping
strings of rainbow drops
from bough to bough.
Tonight
it will dazzle us with lights
and everyone will sing.

Over there
on the edge of the square
rather small, very young
is another tree
snow sprinkled,
twinkling silver
in the sun.
A sparrow sits
on top of it
so proud, so still...
Who will sing to THIS tree?
ME — I WILL!

Constance Levy

Oh, Christmas Tree

Oh, Christmas tree, oh, Christmas tree,
With faithful leaves unchanging;
Oh, Christmas tree, oh, Christmas tree,
With faithful leaves unchanging;
Not only green in summer's heat,
But also winter's snow and sleet,
Oh, Christmas tree, oh, Christmas tree,
With faithful leaves unchanging.

Traditional

In the Week When Christmas Comes

This is the week when Christmas comes.

Let every pudding burst with plums,
And every tree bear dolls and drums,
    In the week when Christmas comes.

Let every hall have boughs of green,
With berries glowing in between,
    In the week when Christmas comes.

Let every doorstep have a song
Sounding the dark street along,
    In the week when Christmas comes.

Let every steeple ring a bell
With a joyful tale to tell,
    In the week when Christmas comes.

Let every night put forth a star
To show us where the heavens are,
    In the week when Christmas comes.

Let every stable have a lamb,
Sleeping warm beside its dam,
    In the week when Christmas comes.

This is the week when Christmas comes.

Eleanor Farjeon

Duckle, Duckle, Daisy

Duckle, duckle, daisy
Martha must be crazy,
She went and made a Christmas cake
Of olive oil and gluten-flake,
And put it in the sink to bake,
Duckle, duckle, daisy.

Leroy F. Jackson

Making Christmas Pudding

Into the basin put the plums,
Stirabout, stirabout, stirabout!

Next the good white flour comes,
Stirabout, stirabout, stirabout!

Sugar and peel and eggs and spice,
Stirabout, stirabout, stirabout!

Mix them and fix them and cook them twice,
Stirabout, stirabout, stirabout!

Traditional

Gingerbread House

We're building a house
of molasses and flour
and sugar and butter —
a house to *devour.*
It's held together with icing
as white as the snow
that's falling
outside tonight.
A gumdrop chimney
and it's complete.
But NOW it looks
too good to eat!

Dee Lillegard

We Wish You a Merry Christmas

We wish you a merry Christmas
And a happy New Year;
A pocket full of money
And a house full of cheer;
And a great fat pig
To last you all the year.

Traditional

FROM *Marmion*

Heap on more wood! — the wind is chill;
But let it whistle as it will,
We'll keep our Christmas merry still.

Sir Walter Scott

An Old English Carol

God bless the master of this house,
Likewise the mistress too.
May their barns be filled with wheat and corn
And their hearts be always true.

Traditional

FROM *The Birds*

A dove settled down in Nazareth.
    Tsucroo!
And tenderly chanted with all his breath.
    Tsucroo!
"O you," he cooed, "so good and true,
my gentleness I'll give to you—
    Tsucroo, Tsucroo, Tsucroo!"

Czechoslovakian carol

Long, Long Ago

Winds through the olive trees
   Softly did blow,
Round little Bethlehem
   Long, long ago.

Sheep on the hillside lay
   Whiter than snow,
Shepherds were watching them,
   Long, long ago.

Then from the happy sky,
   Angels bent low
Singing their songs of joy,
   Long, long ago.

For in a manger bed,
   Cradled we know,
Christ came to Bethlehem,
   Long, long ago.

Anonymous

Shepherd's Song at Christmas

Look there at the star!
I, among the least,
Will arise and take
A journey to the East.
But what shall I bring
As a present for the King?
What shall I bring to the Manger?

> I will bring a song,
> A song that I will sing,
> In the Manger.

Watch out for my flocks,
Do not let them stray.
I am going on a journey
Far, far away.
But what shall I bring
As a present for the Child?
What shall I bring to the Manger?

> I will bring a lamb,
> Gentle, meek, and mild,
> A lamb for the Child
> In the Manger.

I'm just a shepherd boy,
Very poor I am—
But I know there is
A King in Bethlehem.
What shall I bring
As a present just for Him?
What shall I bring to the Manger?

I will bring my heart
And give my heart to Him.
I will bring my heart
To the Manger.

Langston Hughes

Busy

Busy making popcorn balls,
   Busy with the tree,
Busy mailing greeting cards,
   Busy, busy me!

Busy wrapping packages;
   Say, I will be bound—
I'm so busy—I don't see
How Santa gets around!

Leland B. Jacobs

Under the Mistletoe

I did not know she'd take it so,
            Or else I'd never dared:
Although the bliss was worth the blow,
I did not know she'd take it so.
She stood beneath the mistletoe
So long I thought she cared;
I did not know she'd take it so,
Or else I'd never dared.

Countee Cullen

The Twenty-fourth of December

The clock ticks slowly, slowly in the hall,
And slower and more slow the long hours crawl;
It seems as though today
Would never pass away;
The clock ticks slowly, s-l-o-w-l-y in the hall.

Anonymous

Now December's Here

Everything is "secrets"
now December's here:
secrets wrapped in tissue,
whispered in an ear,
secrets big and bulky,
secrets small and slight,
in the strangest places,
hidden out of sight,
packages that rattle,
packages that squeak...
Some say DO NOT OPEN.
Some say DO NOT PEEK.
Secrets, secrets, secrets,
with Christmas coming near.
...except it is no secret
I wish that it were *here*.

Aileen Fisher

A Visit from St. Nicholas

'Twas the night before Christmas, when all through the house
Not a creature was stirring, not even a mouse;
The stockings were hung by the chimney with care,
In hopes that St. Nicholas soon would be there;
The children were nestled all snug in their beds;
While visions of sugarplums danced in their heads;
And mamma in her 'kerchief, and I in my cap,
Had just settled our brains for a long winter's nap—
When out on the lawn there arose such a clatter,
I sprang from my bed to see what was the matter.
Away to the windows I flew like a flash,
Tore open the shutters, and threw up the sash.
The moon, on the breast of the new-fallen snow,
Gave the luster of midday to objects below;

When, what to my wondering eyes should appear,
but a miniature sleigh and eight tiny reindeer,
With a little old driver, so lively and quick,
I knew in a moment it must be St. Nick.
More rapid than eagles his coursers they came,
And he whistled, and shouted, and called them by name:
"Now, *Dasher!* now, *Dancer!* now, *Prancer* and *Vixen!*
On, *Comet!* on, *Cupid!* on, *Donner* and *Blitzen!*
To the top of the porch! to the top of the wall!
Now dash away! dash away! dash away all!"
As dry leaves that before the wild hurricane fly,
When they meet with an obstacle, mount to the sky;
So up to the housetop the coursers they flew
With the sleigh full of toys, and St. Nicholas too.

And then, in a twinkling, I heard on the roof
The prancing and pawing of each little hoof—
As I drew in my head, and was turning around,
Down the chimney St. Nicholas came with a bound.
He was dressed all in fur, from his head to his foot,
And his clothes were all tarnished with ashes and soot;
A bundle of toys he had flung on his back,
And he looked like a pedlar just opening his pack.
His eyes—how they twinkled; his dimples, how merry!
His cheeks were like roses, his nose like a cherry!
His droll little mouth was drawn up like a bow,
And the beard of his chin was as white as the snow;
The stump of a pipe he held tight in his teeth,
And the smoke it encircled his head like a wreath;

He had a broad face and a little round belly
That shook, when he laughed, like a bowl full of jelly.
He was chubby and plump, a right jolly old elf,
And I laughed when I saw him, in spite of myself;
A wink of his eye and a twist of his head
Soon gave me to know I had nothing to dread;
He spoke not a word, but went straight to his work,
And filled all the stockings; then turned with a jerk,
And laying his finger aside of his nose,
And giving a nod, up the chimney he rose;
He sprang to his sleigh, to his team gave a whistle,
And away they all flew like the down of a thistle.
But I heard him exclaim, ere he drove out of sight,
"Happy Christmas to all, and to all a good night!"

Clement Clarke Moore

Merry Christmas

M for the **M**usic, merry and clear;
E for the **E**ve, the crown of the year;
R for the **R**omping of bright girls and boys;
R for the **R**eindeer that bring them the toys;
Y for the **Y**ule log softly aglow.

C for the **C**old of the sky and the snow;
H for the **H**earth where they hang up the hose;
R for the **R**eel which the old folks propose;
I for the **I**cicles seen through the pane;
S for the **S**leigh bells, with tinkling refrain;
T for the **T**ree with gifts all abloom;
M for the **M**istletoe hung in the room;
A for the **A**nthems we all love to hear;
S for **St.** Nicholas—joy of the year!

St. Nicholas Magazine

I Heard the Bells on Christmas Day

I heard the bells on Christmas day
Their old, familiar carols play,
And wild and sweet the words repeat
    Of peace on earth, goodwill to men.

Henry Wadsworth Longfellow

Christmas Present

A candy cane —
an orange —
a walnut in the toe —
Santa filled my stocking.
At least Mom told me so.
But the dollhouse that I found
was not made by an elf.
Grandpa made it just for me —
with love —
by himself.

Bobbi Katz

The Christmas Stocking

Specializes
in those surprises
that come in small sizes.

Dee Lillegard

FROM *The New Year*

I am the little New Year, ho, ho!
Here I come tripping over the snow,
Shaking my bells with a merry din—
So open your doors and let me in!

Anonymous